CHICKEN LITTLE

Rebecca Emberley
and Ed Emberley

Chicken Little was not the brightest chicken in the coop. He was very excitable and prone to foolishness.

One day he was doing nothing, his usual pastime, when an acorn fell from the sky and hit him on the head.

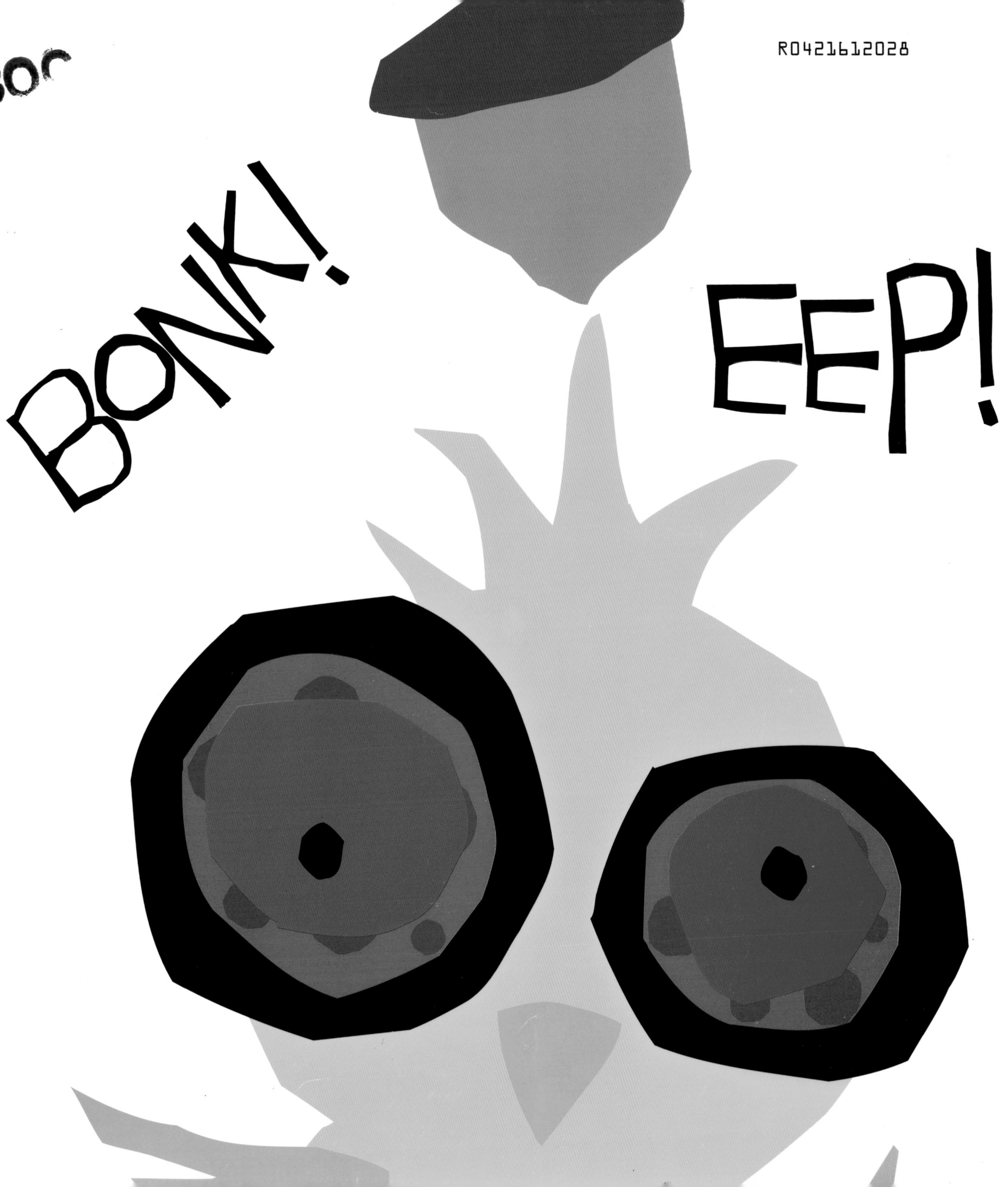
BONK!
EEP!

It knocked him senseless.

"Oh my goodness, oh my gracious!" he exclaimed. "The sky is falling! The sky is falling! I must run for my life!" He grabbed his umbrella to protect his scrambled noggin and ran out into the world without much of a plan.

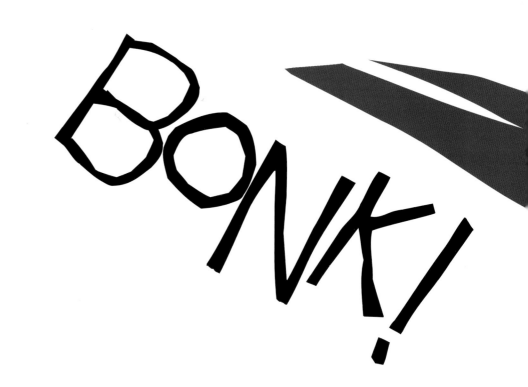

BONK!

It was not long
before he bumped
into Henny Penny.

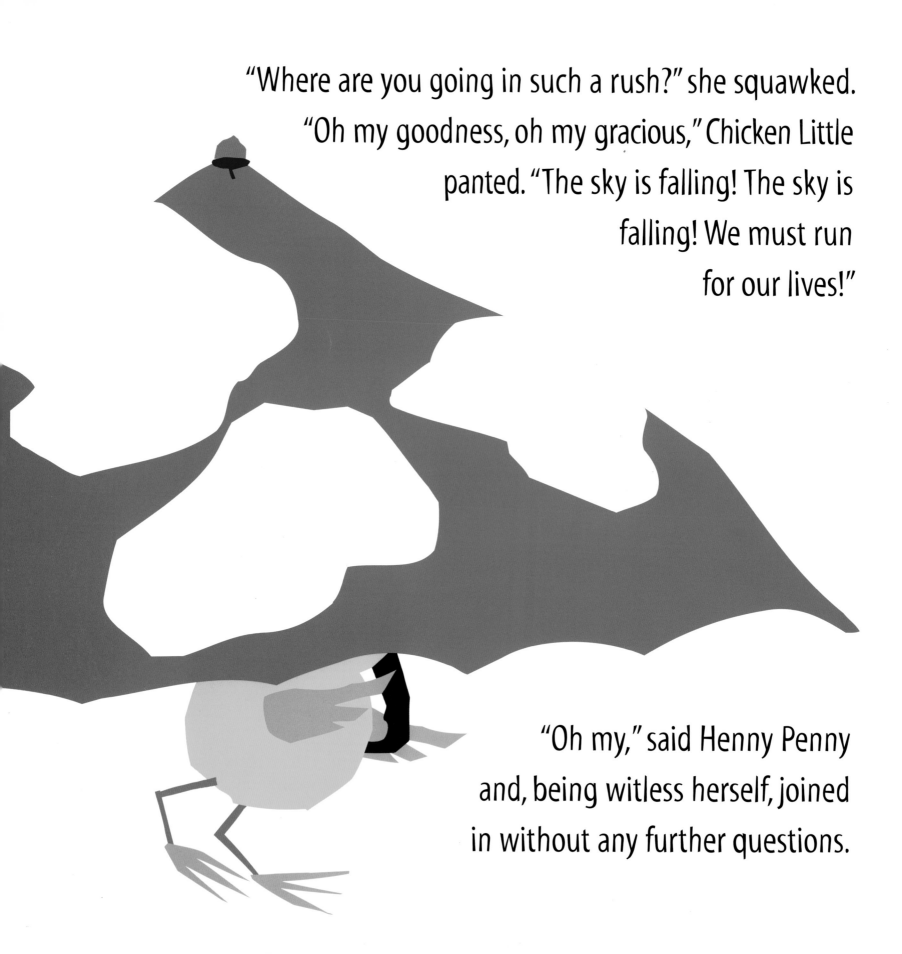

"Where are you going in such a rush?" she squawked. "Oh my goodness, oh my gracious," Chicken Little panted. "The sky is falling! The sky is falling! We must run for our lives!"

"Oh my," said Henny Penny and, being witless herself, joined in without any further questions.

And off they ran.
Still no plan.

Within minutes they ran into Lucky Ducky.

"Hey," he quacked. "Why are you in such a hurry?"

"Oh my goodness, oh my gracious," huffed Chicken Little. "The sky is falling, and we are running for our lives!" Henny Penny could not catch her breath, so she said nothing. Not wanting to be left out, Lucky Ducky joined in, and off they ran. And still no plan.

Momentarily they ran
into Loosey Goosey.
(Honestly, with names
like these, is it any wonder?)

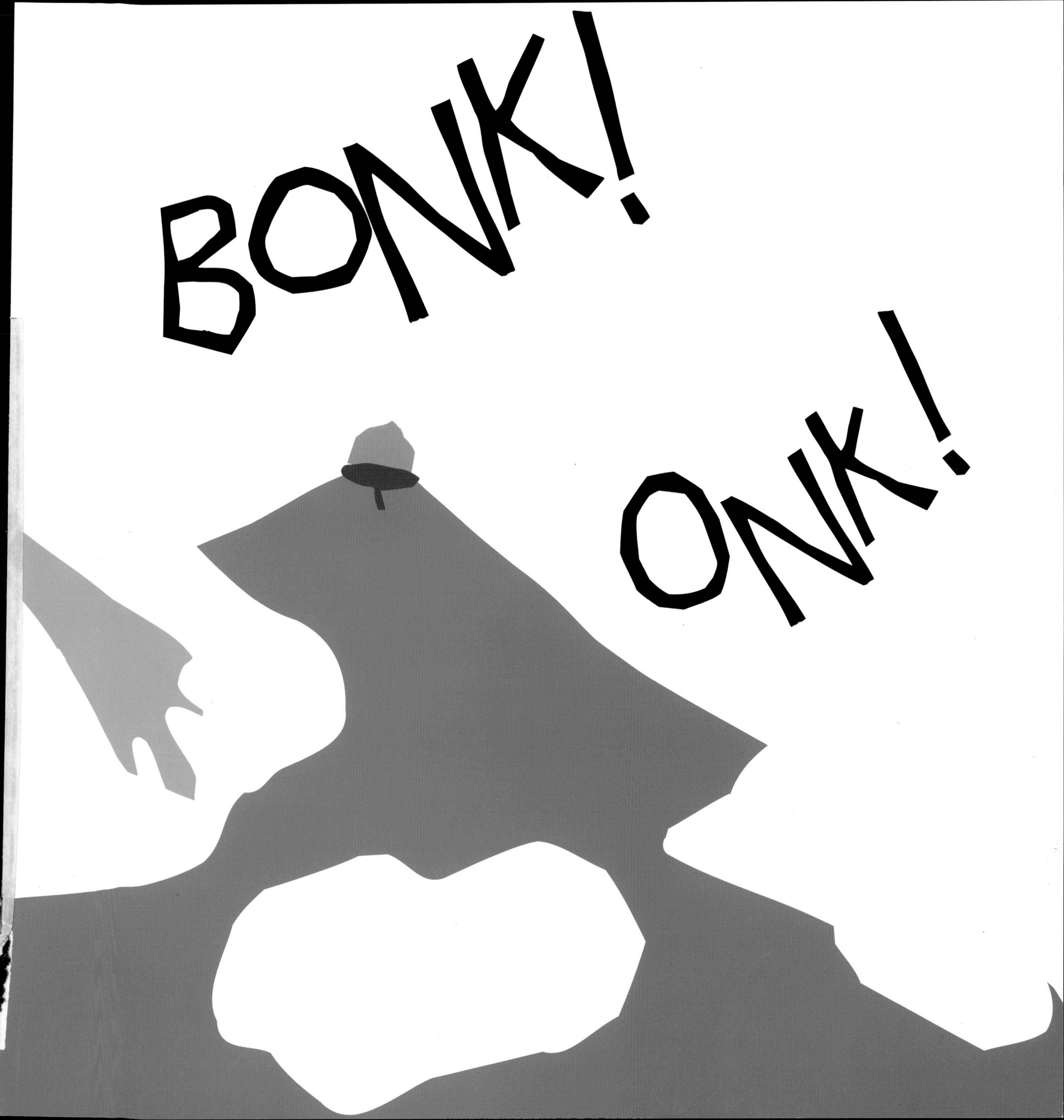
BONK!
ONK!

"Why don't you watch where you're going?" she honked.

"Oh my goodness, oh my gracious," rasped Chicken Little. "The sky is falling, and we are running for our lives!"

"What a bother. I'd better come with you. What's the plan?" asked the goose.

"No time for a plan," they puffed. "The sky is falling!" And off they ran.

As it was growing dark,
they ran into Turkey Lurky.

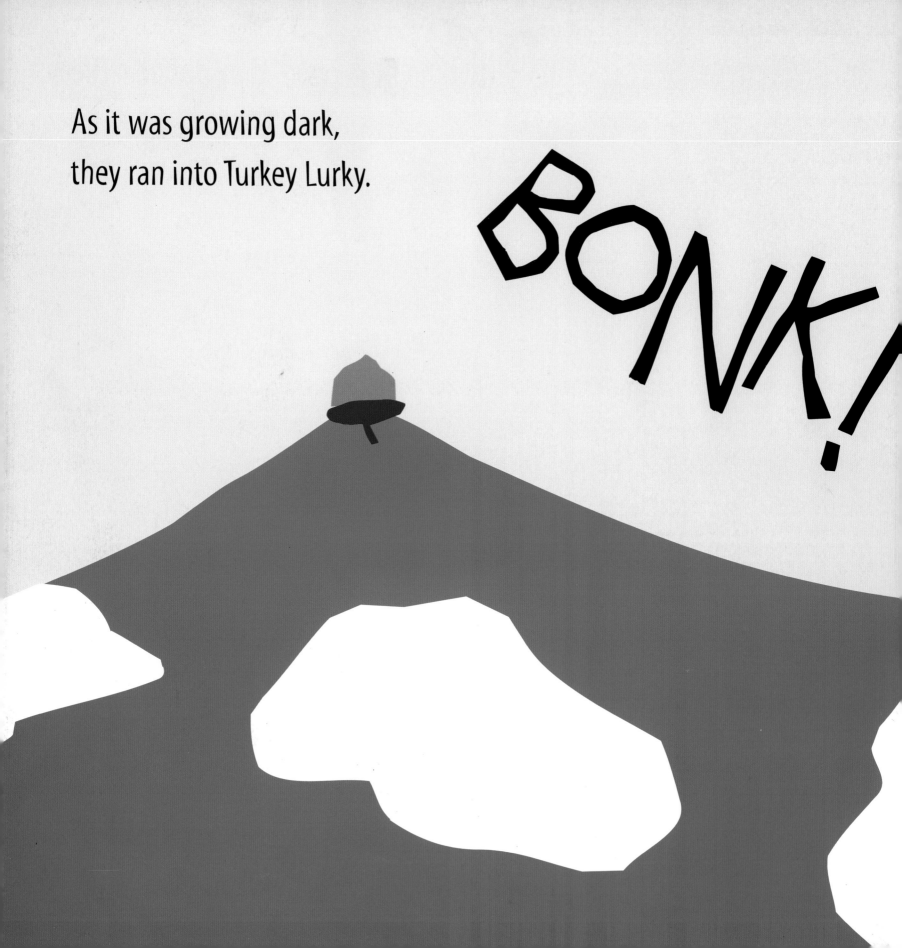

"How dare you!"
he gobbled.

"Oh my goodness, oh my gracious," croaked Chicken Little. "The sky is falling, and we are running for our lives! No time to explain!"
And off they ran.

Soon the anxious little flock grew tired.
They were not used to all this running.
Then they ran into Foxy Loxy . . .

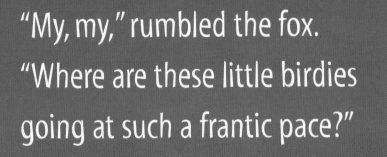

"My, my," rumbled the fox. "Where are these little birdies going at such a frantic pace?"

"Oh my goodness, oh my gracious," gasped Chicken Little, who was now quite out of breath. "The sky is falling, and we are running for our lives!"

"Oh my goodness indeed," said the fox. "We must find a place for you to rest. Step into this warm, dark cave where the sky cannot fall on you."

Without another thought in their tired, feathered heads (oh my gracious!), the flock went forward gratefully into the warm, dark cave.

"Pheeeeew!"
squawked the hen.
"It stinks in here."

"And the floor is squishy and
wet!" quacked the duck.

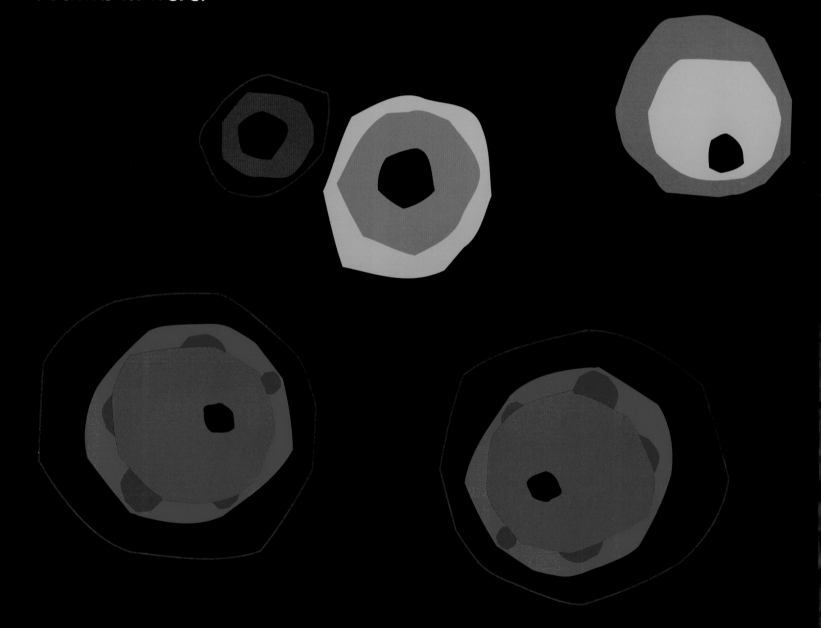

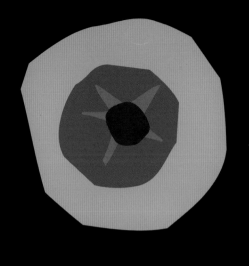
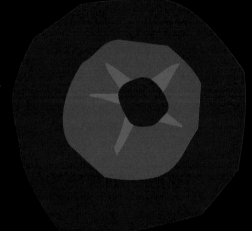
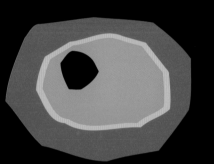

"Uh oh!" gobbled

the turkey.

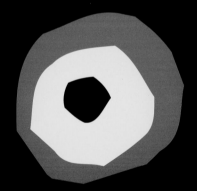
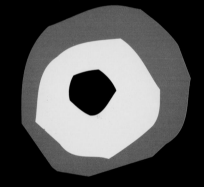

"Oh no!" honked

the goose.

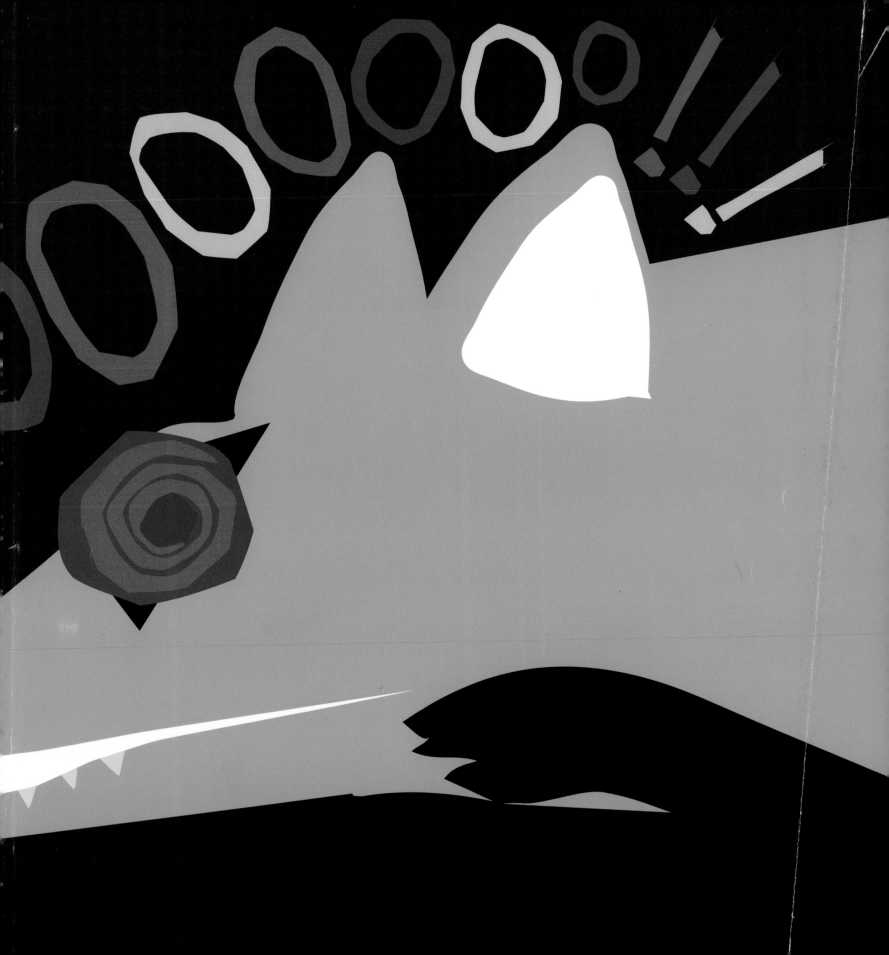

Roaring Brook Press is a division of Holtzbrinck Publishing Holdings Limited Partnership   175 Fifth Avenue, New York, New York 10010
www.roaringbrookpress.com   All rights reserved

Distributed in Canada by H.B. Fenn and Company Ltd.

Library of Congress Cataloging-in-Publication Data
Emberley, Ed.
Chicken Little / Ed Emberley and Rebecca Emberley. — 1st ed.
p. cm.
"A Neal Porter Book."
Summary: A retelling of the classic story of Chicken Little, who has an acorn fall on his head
and runs in a panic to his friends Henny Penny, Lucky Ducky, and Loosey Goosey, to tell them the sky is falling.
ISBN-13: 978-1-59643-464-6   [1. Folklore.] I. Emberley, Rebecca. II. Chicken Licken. III. Title.   PZ8.1.E5725Ch 2009   398.2—dc22   [E]   2008049329

Roaring Brook Press books are available for special promotions and premiums. For details contact: Director of Special Markets, Holtzbrinck Publishers.

First Edition March 2009
Printed in March 2009 in China by South China Printing Company Ltd.,
Dongguan City, Guangdong Province
3 5 7 9 10 8 6 4 2